PEANUTS

Go Fly a Kite, CHARLIE BROWN!

By Charles M. Schulz

Illustrated by Will Yak

story adapted by Cordelia Evans

Simon Spotlight

New York   London   Toronto   Sydney   New Delhi

SIMON SPOTLIGHT
An imprint of Simon & Schuster Children's Publishing Division
1230 Avenue of the Americas, New York, New York 10020
First Simon Spotlight paperback edition May 2015
© 2015 Peanuts Worldwide LLC.
All rights reserved, including the right of reproduction in whole or in part in any form.
SIMON SPOTLIGHT and colophon are registered trademarks of Simon & Schuster, Inc.
For information about special discounts for bulk purchases, please contact Simon & Schuster Special Sales at
1-866-506-1949 or business@simonandschuster.com.
Designed by Ciara Gay
Manufactured in the United States of America 0315 LAK
10 9 8 7 6 5 4 3 2 1
ISBN 978-1-4814-3955-8
ISBN 978-1-4814-3956-5 (eBook)

Today the sky is blue, the sun is shining, and there's a strong breeze. It's the perfect kind of day for Charlie Brown's *favorite* activity.

"Bye, Sally," he tells his sister. "I'm going to go fly a kite!"

Then he grabs his new blue kite and heads outside.

Charlie Brown arrives at an empty field—empty except for one innocent-looking tree.

"You're a kite-eating tree, aren't you?" he asks the tree, but it doesn't respond. Charlie Brown is suspicious, but he's not about to let a tree stop him from flying his kite!

He starts to run with his kite, and just as it is about to catch a gust of wind . . . he feels a sharp tug on the string.

Charlie Brown turns to see what his kite is snagged on, and finds it stuck in the tree's branches.

"Aaugh!" Charlie Brown groans. "I *knew* this was a kite-eating tree!" he shouts. Then he stomps over to the tree to give it a piece of his mind.

"Now, look, tree. That's my kite you've got up there, and I want it back!" he says, shaking his fist. "You can't go grabbing every kite that flies by, you know! Now, give it back. Do you hear me?"

The tree says nothing.
"You can't argue with a kite-eating tree," Charlie Brown says to himself as he begins the sad walk home without his kite.

Charlie Brown gets to work making another kite—a red one this time.
"Back so soon?" Sally asks him.
"I'm hoping the kite-eating tree isn't in the mood for strawberry flavor," Charlie Brown replies as he heads outside with his new kite.
"Everyone likes strawberry flavor," Sally says. "Don't they?"

And sure enough, as soon Charlie Brown starts running with the red kite . . . he feels that familiar tug on the end of the string. The tree has eaten his kite—again!

Now Charlie Brown is really angry. "If you don't let go of that kite," he yells at the tree, "I'll kick you right in the stomach!"

The tree says nothing. So Charlie Brown marches over and kicks its trunk as hard as he possibly can. But the tree still doesn't give up the kite. And now Charlie Brown's foot hurts.

"These kite-eating trees have hard stomachs," he says.

Charlie Brown goes home to make even more kites: yellow, green, and orange ones.

"Why are you making so many kites?" Sally asks.

"It liked the blueberry and the strawberry, and I bet it will like the lemon flavor too," Charlie Brown replies. "But I'd really like to find a flavor it *doesn't* like."

Sally thinks for a moment, then shrugs. "Try the lime green on

The tree says nothing. So Charlie Brown marches over and kicks its trunk as hard as he possibly can. But the tree still doesn't give up the kite. And now Charlie Brown's foot hurts.

"These kite-eating trees have hard stomachs," he says.

Charlie Brown goes home to make even more kites: yellow, green, and orange ones.

"Why are you making so many kites?" Sally asks.

"It liked the blueberry and the strawberry, and I bet it will like the lemon flavor too," Charlie Brown replies. "But I'd really like to find a flavor it *doesn't* like."

Sally thinks for a moment, then shrugs. "Try the lime green on

So Charlie Brown, along with Snoopy, heads back to the field with the yellow and green kites. Snoopy flies the yellow kite while Charlie Brown flies the green kite . . . or tries to, anyway.

The tree quickly eats Charlie Brown's kite, as usual. But he is surprised to see Snoopy flying the yellow kite high up, up, up in the air.

What did you expect? thinks Snoopy. *I'm the World's Greatest Kite Flyer!*

"I guess the tree doesn't like lemon flavor after all," Charlie Brown says. "I need to take note of that."

But when Charlie Brown attempts to fly the yellow kite himself, the tree eats it. The kite-eating tree seems to eat *any* kite Charlie Brown is flying.

"I can't stand it. I just can't stand it!" Charlie Brown exclaims.

Charlie Brown is determined not to feed the kite-eating tree any more kites! He marches up to the tree again and leans in close.

"What would you do if I decided not to fly any more kites this year?" he asks. When he doesn't get a reply, he shouts, "You'd starve to death, that's what you'd do!"

Charlie Brown is still mad, but a small part of him feels better knowing that the tree needs him. *It's nice to be needed*, Charlie Brown thinks to himself.

That's when he runs into Lucy and Linus.

"You hate that tree, don't you, Charlie Brown?" asks Linus.

Charlie Brown nods. "You know why I hate it? Because it's greedy, that's why! Even while it has a kite in its branches, it'll reach out and grab another one! It's like a little kid eating french fries. One is never enough!"

Linus and Lucy decide to check out the kite-eating tree for themselves. "Don't get too close," warns Charlie Brown as they walk away.

When she sees the tree, Lucy gets an idea. *If the kite-eating tree eats kites, maybe it also eats dirty blue baby blankets that certain little brothers need to stop carrying everywhere,* she thinks.

"I don't want to live in a world where kite-eating trees exist," says Linus sadly, as he looks up at the pieces of kite poking out of the tree.

That's when Lucy takes his blanket . . .

. . . and feeds it to the kite-eating tree, which gobbles it right up.

Linus stands in shock for a moment. "My own sister threw my blanket up in a kite-eating tree!" he wails, and runs to Charlie Brown and Snoopy to ask for help.

Snoopy immediately puts on his Rescue Squad hat.

"Here comes the captain of the Rescue Squad!" shouts Charlie Brown. "He's going to save Linus's blanket!"

"That silly beagle won't be able to save anything," says Lucy as Snoopy starts to climb the trunk of the tree. "Beagles can't climb trees!"

We can't? thinks Snoopy.

He continues to try to climb the tree anyway. He makes it about halfway up before he realizes Lucy is right.

Why am I doing this? he thinks as he slides to the ground with a loud *thud!*

"Now I'll never get my blanket back!" cries Linus. "Just like Charlie Brown has never gotten a kite back!"

"Stand back, everyone," Lucy says, exasperated. "I'll get your silly blanket back." Then she yells up at the kite-eating tree, "You give that blanket back right now, do you hear me? It may be dumb and babyish, but it's my brother's, and I shouldn't have let you eat it!"

The tree shudders and Linus's blanket falls out, along with several old, chewed-up kites.

"I thought I'd never see my blanket again," says Linus, hugging it close.

"Look, Charlie Brown, there's one good kite left!" Linus exclaims, pointing to a perfectly shaped kite in the pile of mangled ones.

"You're right!" says Charlie Brown. "But . . . there's no more wind to fly it in."

Snoopy has an idea . . . and calls on Woodstock and the Beagle Scouts to help him with it.